CULLODEN

JOANNE AUSTEN BROWN

Culloden
Joanne Austen Brown

Title: Culloden

Copyright © 2023 Joanne Austen Brown

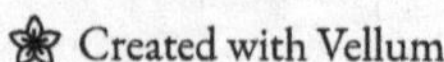 Created with Vellum

Books By Joanne Austen Brown

Always Louisa ~ Book One: Always Series

Always Elspeth ~ Book Two: Always Series

Always Delia ~ Book Three: Always Series

Rachael's Jaunt ~ Book One: Come with Me

Molly's Laird ~ Book Two: Come with Me

Novellas

The Secret Letter

A Partridge in His Family Tree

To my readers who take time out to read my books.

CULLODEN

'History is dead.' There, she said it. But she meant it even though she had not wanted to say anything until they had gotten home from their vacation. And this tour.

Her dad was staring at her. The shock on his face was real. He was holding on to his temper that much Jesse could see. He did not look happy.

'But Dad...it is.' Jesse frowned, looking northward. She did not want to meet her dad's gaze.

'I won't say this again, I don't care what you think. This is the next part of the tour. You can't stay on the bus. So, get into the museum and stay out of trouble.'

Stomping down the bus steps, backpack in hand, Jesse made a beeline across the carpark for the main doors of the Culloden Museum. She could hear the footsteps of her dad as he followed but she would not look back. She loved history and always had. But this was way too much. For days and days, they had been travelling by bus going from one battlefield to another, one castle to another, to museums and statues. Now, they were all one in her mind. A great big jumble. It all felt the same. She'd had enough. History was dead. No one could get any more out of it. If this was all it could offer, she wanted no more of it. She was so over it.

She entered the museum with her dad close behind her. The rest of the tour participants scattered around, watching her. Her head dipped for a second. They looked just as annoyed as her dad. They didn't seem to think much of her, and the feelings were mutual. She wandered around stopping every now and then to look at something. All the time she felt her father's eyes upon her. She did love history. She was being selfish and childish. She just couldn't stop herself. Seems a seventeen-year-old can act like a child.

Jesse found a corner where she could see the group go out of the museum and into the battlefield. It was near the great expanse of glass window that looked out across the field. A haunting view. She plopped herself down on the floor, pulling her beanie down, almost covering her eyes. Pulling a book from her backpack, she began leafing through it. A book of the history of this place. Culloden. Maybe they would let her sit in the corner and read, while they went out into the field. Jesse watched the main group follow the tour guide out the door onto the 'field of battle'. Her dad was looking at her with frustration etched on his face. Then he threw his hands up in despair and walked out the door. Even some of the other tourists were frowning at her. Her dad had spent ages putting this tour together for her, showing her the parts of Scotland that he believed would enthral her. The Scotland her dad loved and that she had thought she loved too. She did love it but seeing the same thing over and over. Aghh. What more could they learn from history?

Giving a huge sigh of reluctance, Jesse got up and made her way to the end of the line. Putting the book in her backpack, she followed the group, aware that she was being more than childish. She was downright selfish. She knew she had to 'pull her head in'.

It was cool outside, so she pulled the zip of her jacket up and threw the backpack onto her shoulders. Walking past most of the group, she headed for the open field following the path that led into the mist. She still wanted to be alone, but she would remain in sight of the group so that her dad wouldn't worry. She shook her head. She had behaved in a ridiculous manner. She felt the tourists' stares drill into her back as she walked away.

Watching her feet rather than where she was going, she wandered down the path as the mist grew thicker around her. After a minute or two she lifted her head to see that the mist had surrounded her completely. She could hear the chatter from the tour group but could no longer see them. The sound was muffled and distant. She turned around, wanting to spot them. But the mist hid all, it was swirling around her. She didn't care. She didn't have to look at their disapproving faces. She could be on her own regardless of how silly she was feeling.

The mist was dense, colourless and lifeless. Looking around, she could only just make out the path and the many small and larger stones that lay on either side of it. They were natural stones but placed in various sizes around the path and toward the end a much bigger monument of stone. It was big and dark, and she assumed they were made of stones similar to the ones scattered around the path.

From the corner of her eye, she saw a dash of red. But then it was gone. It was probably nothing. No. There it was again. A flash of red, black, cream. Were they black straps? Were these people part of the tour group? Suddenly, people in uniforms materialised before her in the mist. British soldiers, British soldiers from the 18th century formed up together on her right.

Okay, this would be better than she first thought. They have reenactors. That would add a bit of life to the place. She looked around and found a rock on which she sat down. Some of the stones were too big to sit on but she had found one that was perfect. Pulling off her beanie, she let her dark hair cascade down her back. She would enjoy this and have the best view. She looked around. Where was her dad? If only he could see her happiness and the smile on her face now. Placing her back-pack next to her, she got comfortable on the smallish stone.

The mist to her left was swirling now and colour starting to take shape. Men in kilts but not the modern ones like you see on TV or you could get in the tourist shops in Edinburgh. Proper historical kilts that men wrapped around them. They had various examples in the museum. Kilts, legs, boots and shoes. Old and muddy. Bearded men, even young boys. They were doing this enactment properly. Everything looked authentic to her untrained eyes.

She marvelled at the enactors as the group of Scots on her left, united. Kilts of dirty red and blue with lines of other colours flowing through them. Yellow, pale blue and muddy brown. Actually, most of the men had a good layer of muddy brown all over them. She loved the beards. Old ones, long ones, red and brown ones. She examined each figure. The shape of the heads, legs, their kilts and swords. The multitude of colours. Then she looked at the British to her right, who to her all looked the same in their flaming red jackets.

With no sign or sound of a beginning they were fighting. Hand to hand, sword to sword and gun to gun. Gunshots could be heard and the clanging of the swords on the shields. She heard the pounding of the drums. Battle cries and yells. Wow this was fantastic and so lifelike.

The actors were throwing themselves into their perfor-mance. It all looked so real. But something was wrong. That looked like real blood. Her stomach began to ache. She could smell blood and the sweat. She could feel the heat and the tension in the air. Her breath stuck in her throat. This was no act. This was real. But that couldn't be. She had to get out of here. She tried to move but was frozen in place. This was real and she wanted to scream. No sound came out of her mouth. Sudden heat enveloped her, and she too was hot and sweaty.

A Scot fell to his knees in front of her. He was young and handsome. He had to be only twenty or so. Blood poured from a stomach wound as he reached up with his sword and guttered the British soldier who had slashed him. The British soldier fell to the ground and did not move. The young Scot was dying, and she could see it. His eyes looked directly at her. Her gaze froze. She could not look away. His beautiful face went white as the life drained from him. He had no focus, no sight. He was gone. She wanted to cry and scream. Tears rolled down her face, but she could not make a sound. In an instant his face was replaced by a skull. No flesh, no colour, no life. He dropped to the ground, a mere skeleton. Dead. This was horror itself.

Jesse clung to the rock on which she sat. Unable to move as her knuckles grew whiter with her grip. She looked around and the battle continued to rage. Then back to the Scot who had died in front of her. He was whole again but still dead. What was happening? He was dead, a skeleton but a moment ago. Now, he had flesh and blood oozed from his wound. She wiped the tears from her face but could not stop them flowing.

More men, both Scots and British were dying around her. And suddenly they all stopped. Pulling themselves up straight, even the dead, they began to move toward her. Tentatively she reached out to the young man in front of her, the one she had seen die. He was kneeling in front of her. Waiting. She touched him. His face was cold and lifeless. She looked away and saw all the men gazing at her, their kilts and coats gently moving in the breeze. They moved closer and she heard their movements, the clicking of swords against each other, boots of leather creaking. Then they stood still. Only the light howl of the wind could be heard.

If she had wanted to move, it would have been impossible. They surrounded her. Every pair of eyes examining her. Waiting. Looking for something? Recognition? What had she just witnessed?

They were real men or had been. Real men, real soldiers. They had fought this battle many years ago and had come back to show her the real flesh and blood men. No re-enactment. This was history real and true. In front of her. She knew it to be true.

As if having achieved what they had wanted they all as one turned and drifted back into the mist. They were but colours in the mist again. Reds and brown. And finally, they disappeared completely from her sight.

Jesse had no idea how long she sat there, staring into the space to which they had gone. Hours, minutes, moments. Tears still rolled down her cheeks. The touch of a cold soldier still on her fingertips. These soldiers had been real men and had wanted to show her that history was far from dead or unimportant. More than mere words in a book.

The mist was gone, and she heard footsteps come up behind her. She stood and turned then threw herself in her father's arms. She held him hard and close.

'I see now. I see. I'm sorry.' She clung to her dad, silently weeping now that she knew what had happened to her. Finally letting go, she looked at her dad.

Her father said nothing. He wiped the tears from her face. Could she tell him what she had just witnessed? He smiled at her and pointed to the stone that she had been sitting on. There were stones all around her. Names of clan who had fought in this battle. Stewarts, Camerons, MacLauchlans, and Mackintosh's. Jesse looked down at the stone that she had sat on.

A chill went through her, and a gasp left her lips. There in big letters was the name Fraser. She clung to her dad's hand as they walked back down the path toward the museum. There was so much she had to tell. The soldiers she had seen were Frasers. Jesse Fraser would never be the same again. History was real. It had happened.

About the Author

Joanne loves to write and she loves to travel. She is married to Andrew and lives in Central New South Wales Australia with him and their two cats Arthur and Oscar. (Meet them on Joanne's webpage) She has two grown sons and four beautiful granddaughters. Her imagination loves to take her on various trips but mainly in the area of the regency romance.

She also loves meeting new people so do drop a line to her on:

Website Facebook Instagram Twitter

ACKNOWLEDGEMENT

Culloden is a real labour in love. Except it was not a labour. It was pure joy. I first wrote this story for a Rainforest Writers Retreat Ghost Anthology in 2020 after a retreat in 2019 on Ghosts. Unfortunately, my story was mixed up and did not come out the way I had intended. So, I had to revisit it and write it again. This beautiful example is what has eventuated. I love it. It is in many ways the feelings I had when I visited the site myself. I just loved being there. Culloden, my Culloden.

You could if you wanted to, sit on the Fraser rock. The others are two big or two unusual. Fraser was perfect for me.

I also want to acknowledge the following:

To Danielle, my wonderful designer. You know my heart and the beautiful cover proves that.

To Nas, my fantastic editor who loves my stories and gives me her time when I need her. I love that you love my work. As you said this story is powerful and I agree.

To my hubby, Andrew, who gives me the chance to sit and dream of my stories. You never push and never doubt what I do. Thank you.

And to my readers, this is a gift in many ways to you because you want me to keep writing. Thank you.

Joanne

From the Author

I have loved using folk law and traditional history in this series. It has spurred my imagination. I love the way the fae have developed in the story and that they too are not perfect and can give a few bad apples to history.

Having mixed marriages was an idea which was there from the beginning but the fae blood would only appear in the females. That too was my idea and I loved playing with it. If you have loved this story, then you will definitely not want to miss the final in the series "Glenna's Future". And please tell your friends about this series.

Keep a look out for it. It will appear later this year.

And just to tempt you here is the cover...

Go to my website and subscribe to my newsletter. It is only monthly so you won't be bombarded by emails.

https://www.joanneaustenbrown.com/

or join me on my Facebook page.

https://www.facebook.com/joanne.boog/

More Books by Joanne Austen Brown

Always Louisa (Always Series Book 1)

Louisa Stapleton has been disgraced and banished from society. She wants to return to defend herself and seize the life she desires. Her father has obtained the help of the one man she sees as her nemesis. Arriving at the house party, she has her doubts about her success in returning.

Chalanor Farraday, the Viscount Lightford, had a hand in her downfall but he was not a willing participant. To redeem his honour he wants to help her back into the society that rejected her. But she hates him. That is the last thing he wants. Can he convince her to trust him?

Can they overcome the trials that they will face so that Louisa can obtain more than she had hoped for? Neither see the figures lurking in the shadows. They want to prevent her return to society. And they have their reasons for wanting her dead. Will they succeed?

ALWAYS ELSPETH (ALWAYS SERIES BOOK 2)

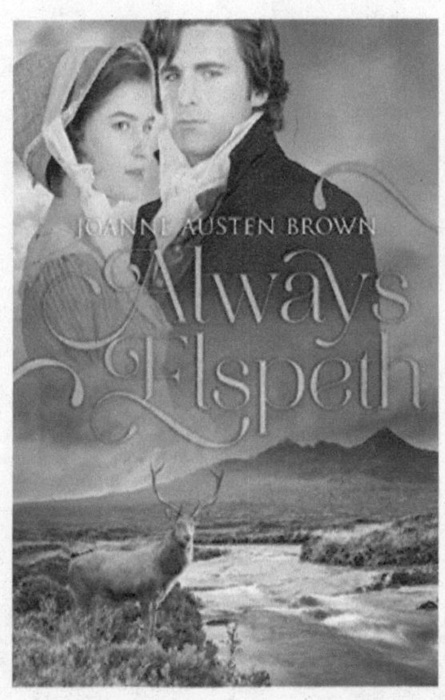

Tragedy has followed Elspeth. Hoping for a new life she moves to the Isle of Skye. Can the society that she hates leave her to start again? What she cannot see is someone who is following her.

James has loved her all his life. Elspeth rejected him once but now she may be tempted to try love again. But in the shadows, someone is stalking her.

Can James and Elspeth renew the love they once had? And make it stronger? Or will the darkness overtake them?

Always Delia (Always Series Book 3)

Delia has been in search for a man she believes is her real father. However, she has been unable to find him. Was her mother telling the truth? Delia decides to go home to the man who raised her and a brother who has protected her.

Lucas has loved Delia almost from the first moment they

met. He has done all that he could to help her find her real father. But now he has, he wants to protect her from a man who he knows she will not want to meet.

Their families have been caught up in a twisted tale of love, loss, and villainy. Now they have a chance at real love and a happy ever after. Will it be for Delia and Lucas?

Rachael's Jaunt
(Come with Me
Book 1)

Rachael Fielding loves Scotland. She escapes her busy life for some down time but does not expect that time to be in 1822. Is she dreaming? And why is the man she knows as her dream Scotsman suddenly there in front of her?

Duncan Murray is a laird though he does not want to be. But he was born to the position. Then Rachael shows up and his world is turned upside down. Can she be the love of his life and what have the Fae got to do with it?

Is she a spy for the soon to visit, King George 4th? Can he believe her stories of the future? The two will be tested to their limits. Will the Fae have their way and is there a future for Duncan and Rachael?

Molly's Laird (Come with Me)

In her own time Molly is a fish out of water. But when she goes back in time to find some peace, after the deaths of all her family, she finds a new beginning.

Can all the promises of the past be true? What about the Fae? And can this handsome man be just for her?

Alasdair misses his brother but understands why he left. He is now Laird but is lonely. Will he find love like Duncan did? Who is the real Molly he cannot stop thinking of? Is she the answer to all he has been searching for? What are the Fae up to?

A Partridge in His Family Tree

Dianna Partridge rejected him, so he became a rake. But Jason Baird wants to settle down. He needs a woman not a simpering Miss.

Dianna has been running her father business, despite being a woman, and very well. But she feels she has missed out on some things.

Can these two get together and have a memorable Christmas?

THE SECRET LETTER

Cora Fitzgibbon appears cold and uninteresting except To Thomas Wright.

He foolishly agrees to be part of a Secret Letter plan invented by his brother. Cold Cora is his match.

But she is not cold or distant and he is very much attracted to her. How can he win her love and keep his promise to his brother.

Love is in the air as Christmas approaches.

Glenna's Future

Coming later in 2023